AWFUL OGRE'S AWFUL DAY

POEMS BY
Jack Prelutsky

PICTURES BY
Paul O. Zelinsky

SCHOLASTIC INC.

New York Toronto London Auckland Sydney
Mexico City New Delhi Hong Kong Buenos Aires

For Jesse Wilks
—J.P.

For Dorothy and David,
Benjamin and Ellen
—P. O. Z.

ISBN 0-439-43794-6

Text copyright © 2001 by Jack Prelutsky.
Illustrations copyright © 2001 by Paul O. Zelinsky. All rights reserved.
Published by Scholastic Inc., 557 Broadway, New York, NY 10012,
by arrangement with Greenwillow Books, an imprint of HarperCollins
Publishers. SCHOLASTIC and associated logos are trademarks
and/or registered trademarks of Scholastic Inc.

12 11 10 9 8 7 6 5   3 4 5 6 7/0

Printed in the U.S.A.   08

First Scholastic printing, September 2002

Watercolors and pen and ink were used for the full-color art.

The text type is Cochin Bold.

CONTENTS

AWFUL OGRE RISES

My rattlesnake awakens me,
I swat its scaly head.
My buzzard pecks my belly
Till I fling it from the bed.
My rats attack me as I rise
But scatter when I roar.
I boot my sweet tarantula
Across the stony floor.

I tickle my piranha,
Who rewards me with a bite,
Then disengage the leeches
That besiege me overnight.
I flick aside the lizard
Clinging grimly to my chin,
And now I feel I'm ready
For my morning to begin.

AWFUL OGRE GROOMS HIMSELF

Another day has started,
I stretch and yawn and shout,
Then rap my cudgel on my skull
To shake the cobwebs out.
I scratch my chest and belly,
My neck and knobby knees,
Then knock my head against the wall
To agitate my fleas.

I snort and grunt and rearrange
Some bones upon a shelf,
Then gaze into the mirror
And commence to groom myself.
I rinse my mouth with onion juice
And dab some on my chin,
I rub my cheeks with dragon blood
To uglify my skin.

I brush my hair with gargoyle oil
That's specially refined,
Then scrub my face with weasel grease,
The extra smelly kind.
When it's apparent I've achieved
My usual appeal,
I trudge into the kitchen
To prepare my morning meal.

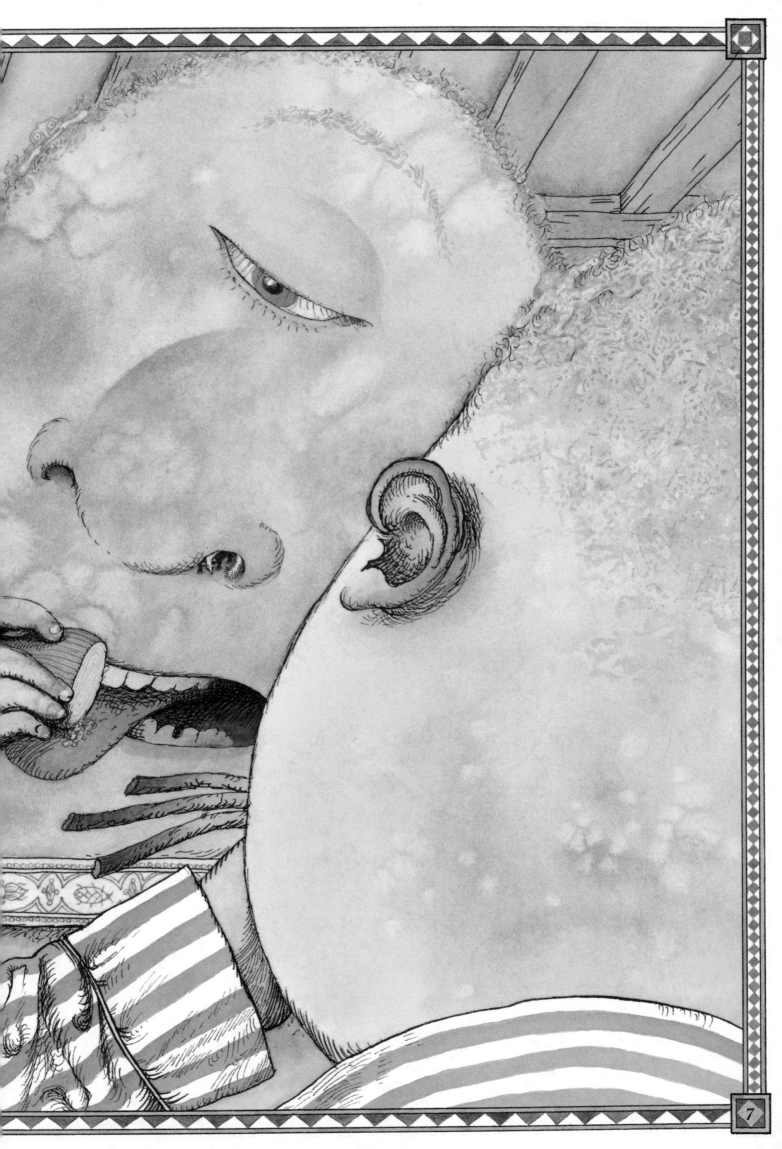

AWFUL OGRE'S BREAKFAST

Oh breakfast, lovely breakfast,
You're the meal I savor most.
I sip a bit of gargoyle bile
And chew some ghoul on toast.

I linger over scrambled legs,
Complete with pickled feet,
Then finish with a piping bowl
Of steamy *SCREAM OF WHEAT*.

AWFUL OGRE AND THE STORM

A storm has arrived without warning
As morning has hardly begun.
A legion of clouds in dark armor
Eclipses the sad little sun.
The temperature drops by the second,
The sky grows increasingly dark.
The neighborhood birds have turned silent,
Every last miserable lark.

Now tentative raindrops are falling,
An ominous wind starts to blow.
The air fills with thunder and lightning,
Announcing this tempest will grow.
The rain is cascading in torrents,
It's soaking the goblins and trolls.
The goblins retreat to their hovels,
The trolls hurry off to their holes.

The thunder grows louder and louder,
The wind topples tree after tree,
As lightning bolts flash ever faster,
Though none have the nerve to touch me.
I stand all alone in the downpour,
So drenched I'm delighted to say,
"What a glorious day for an ogre!
What a glorious, glorious day!"

AWFUL OGRE DANCES

I'm one awful ogre
Who knows how to dance,
And frequently does
In the forest expanse.
I often begin
When I get out of bed,
And move to the music
That swims in my head.

I dance out-of-doors
In my bare ogre feet,
With intricate steps
No one else can repeat.
I dance over mountains,
I dance into town,
I dance right side up,
And I dance upside down.

I dance with abandon,
Bravura, and zest,
I carom off boulders
And beat on my chest.
I pirouette wildly
And leap into space
With power, panache,
And unparalleled grace.

I've danced with a goblin,
A troll, and an elf,
But I dance my best
When I dance by myself.
I dance in my garden
Of hazardous plants—
I'm one awful ogre
Who knows how to dance.

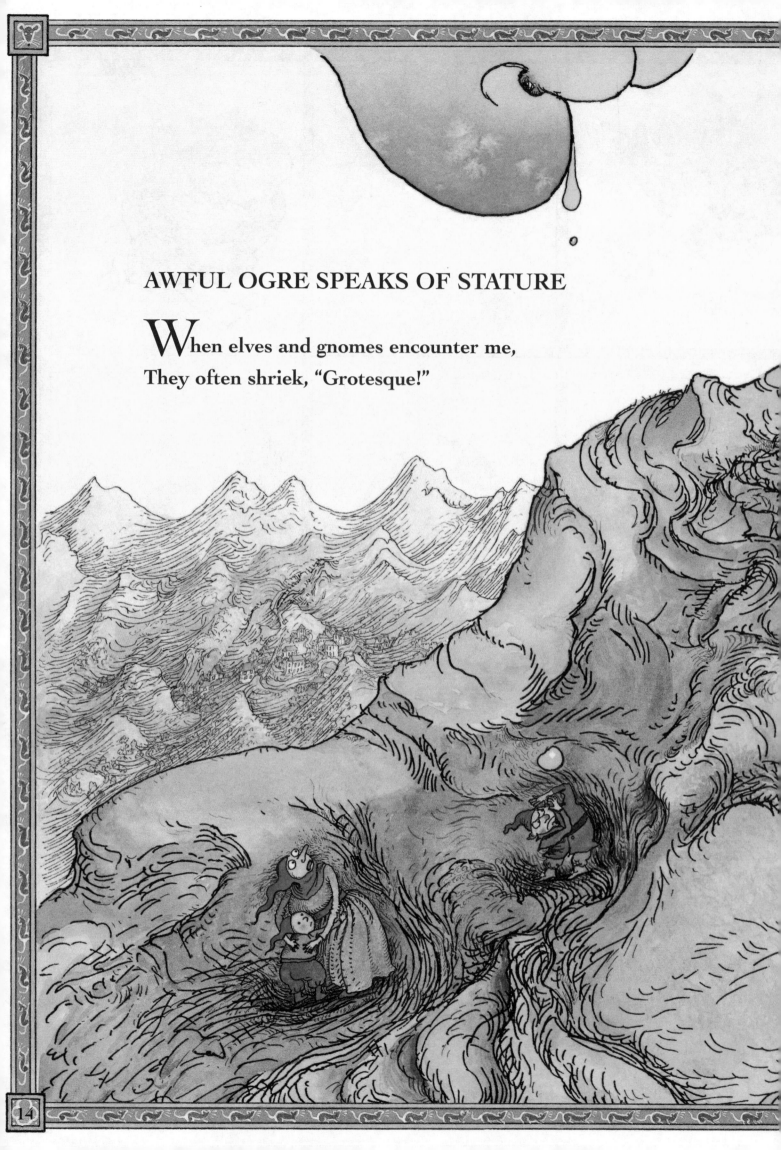

AWFUL OGRE SPEAKS OF STATURE

When elves and gnomes encounter me,
They often shriek, "Grotesque!"

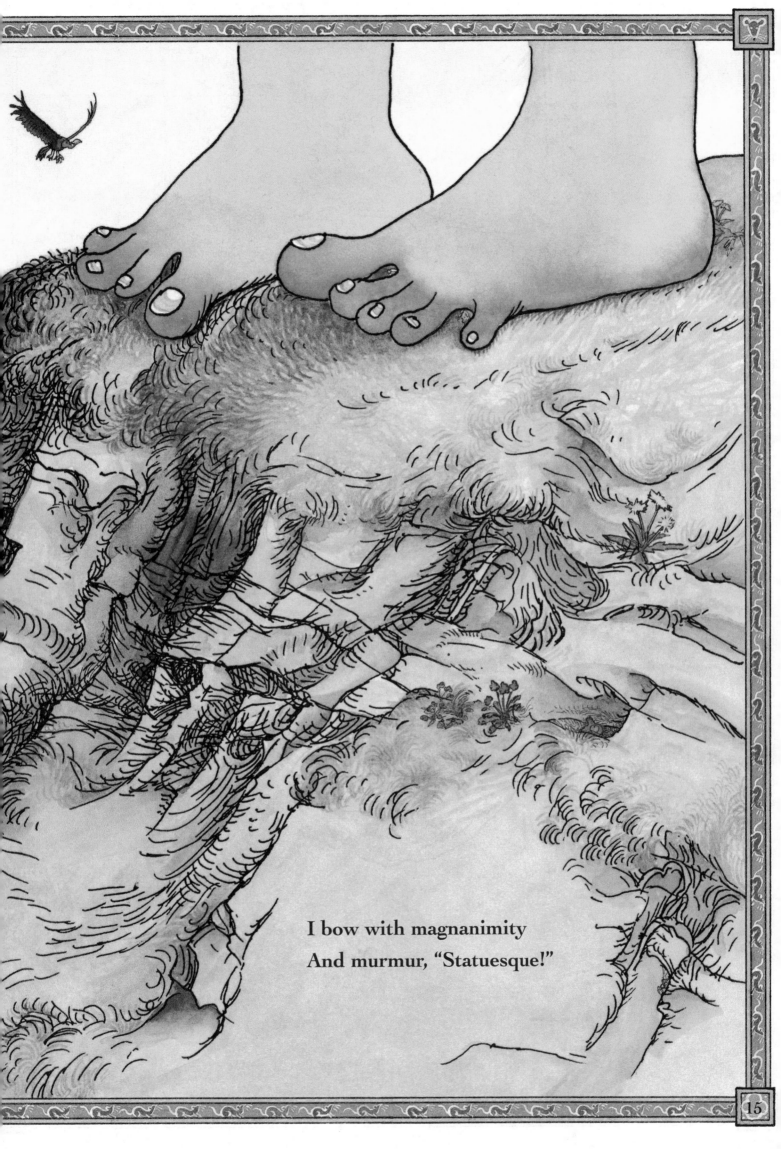

I bow with magnanimity
And murmur, "Statuesque!"

AWFUL OGRE PENS A LETTER

Oh ogress, fair ogress,
Dear ogress divine,
I utterly love you
And wish you were mine.
I long for the sight
Of your craggy gray face,
The might of your bone-breaking,
Painful embrace.

I cherish the touch
Of your sandpaper hands,
The scent of your tresses,
Those greasy green strands.
I treasure the claws
On your fingers and toes,
Your big bloodshot eye,
And your pendulous nose.

You're truly perfection,
Demure and petite,
Just fourteen-foot-four
From your head to your feet.
Your screechy sweet voice
Sends a chill down my spine.
I'll always adore you,
Dear ogress divine.

AWFUL OGRE'S MUSIC

I'm fond of most things musical,
And almost every day
I take my bass and xylophone
And jubilantly play.
I tend to play them both at once
In unrelated keys,
While rapturously singing
Stirring ogre melodies.

I love to trill the highest notes
That make the forest ring.
I love to boom the lowest notes
That only I can sing.
I blare enthusiastically,
I've got no vocal peers.
I give the goblins earaches,
Even drive the trolls to tears.

Some days I'm less exuberant
And simply sit and hum,
Or putter with percussion
On my little bongo drum.
I made it from a hollow log
And moldy melon rind—
I may be an awful ogre,
But I'm musically inclined.

AWFUL OGRE'S HOT DOG LUNCH

I went out for a hot dog lunch
And sat beside a dragon.
We gobbled hot dogs by the bunch,
Then ate the hot dog wagon.

AWFUL OGRE'S VISITOR

He's visiting this afternoon,
And I can hardly wait,
For every time he visits
Is a time to celebrate.
Except for my piranha,
All my pets ran off today . . .
They heard his footfalls thunder
From a hundred miles away.

When he was here a year ago,
We had a grand old time.
We gorged on bowls of roasted troll,
Prepared in special slime.
He boxed my ears repeatedly,
I bit his bulbous nose.
We yanked each other's eyebrow,
And we stomped each other's toes.

No sooner does he see me
Than he socks me on the chin.
We then commence to wrestle,
It takes hours for me to win.
He loves to swing his cudgel
Up and down and left and right,
Demolishing my furniture . . .
He's truly a delight.

He's apt to catch me unawares
And launch a sneak attack.
He bops me soundly on the bean,
Of course I bop him back.
He's just about as big as me
And practically as loud—
He's my great-grandnephew ogre,
And he makes me very proud!

AWFUL OGRE BOASTS A BIT

I'm an awful, awful ogre,
Absolutely awful ogre.
I'm so awful, Awful Ogre
Is my awful ogre name.
Though I know of other ogres
Who are also awful ogres,
I put all those awful ogres
Unequivocally to shame.

I am awful in the morning,
I am awful in the evening,
I am awful every solitary
Second in between.
All the other awful ogres
Know I'm such an awful ogre
That those other awful ogres
Often turn an awful green.

I am awful when it's sunny,
Snowy, cloudy, windy, rainy.
I am awful, awful, awful
Summer, winter, spring, and fall.
"You are awful, Awful Ogre!"
Roar the other awful ogres—
I alone am Awful Ogre,
And the awfulest of all.

AWFUL OGRE'S TV TIME

Some days I like to hunker down
And switch on my TV,
To watch THE OGRE LOGGER
Try to chop a fossil tree.
Then AN OGRESS IN THE KITCHEN
Chops some innards in a pot,
Followed by KARATE OGRES,
Who routinely chop a lot.

Next THE OGRE CHOP COLLECTORS
Show some samples hung on nails,
Chops of lizards, chops of wizards,
And enormous chops of whales.
Then those cartoon BABY OGRES
Chop their dinners with a spoon—
I adore The Chopping Channel
On a lazy afternoon.

AWFUL OGRE
IN THE GARDEN

I'm tending my wonderful garden,
It's several centuries old.
I'm growing carnivorous roses
And oceans of overblown mold.
I lovingly stroke every bramble
And sharpen each perilous thorn
With skills often drilled into ogres
Soon after those ogres are born.

Wherever you are in my garden,
There's something to give you a fright.
My thistles are longing to sting you,
My blossoms are likely to bite.
A number of shrubs may detain you
With tendrils that smother and choke,
While others are openly toxic . . .
My sweet poison ivy and oak.

Because of my ramshackle patches
Where scrofulous weeds rule unchecked,
I've earned from the trolls and the goblins
A measure of grudging respect.
The sight of disease-laden nettles
Arrayed by my blight-ridden pool
Evokes such delight in most ogres,
They mightily holler and drool.

"How utterly wretched!" they bellow.
"How dreadful! How drab! How divine!
Your venomous vines are so thrilling,
They chill every ogreish spine."
The OGRE GREEN GARDEN ALLIANCE
Adores all the flora I grow—
I've now won their medal of honor
For ninety-nine years in a row.

AWFUL OGRE TAKES HIS SUPPER

When I don't feel like cooking,
And supper time is near,
I step out to a restaurant
Just forty miles from here.
No matter if they're crowded,
They always seat me first,
Then bring me pails of water
To alleviate my thirst.

I never need a menu,
They empty every pot
And rush me triple portions
Of everything they've got.
Should that prove insufficient,
I simply start to roar . . .
They whip up extra helpings
And serve me more and more.

I wolf down all they proffer
Till not a scrap remains.
The other patrons notice,
But none of them complains.
They gaze in fascination
As I savor every bite,
Feeling privileged to witness
My titanic appetite.

When the kitchen cannot muster
Even one more drop of broth,
I polish off the silverware,
The plates, and tablecloth.
The waiters stay attentive,
They bow extremely low.
It's patently apparent
That they hate to see me go.

They smile and wave profusely
As I slowly stride away.
They appreciate my business,
And I never have to pay.
My appearance and demeanor
Seem to give me extra clout—
It's ideal to be an ogre
When it comes to dining out.

AWFUL OGRE
REFLECTS ON ATHLETICS

When I was a youngster,
I harbored a dream
Of being the star
Of a basketball team.
My shooting was aimless,
My passing a joke.
Whenever I dribbled,
The basketball broke.

I went out for football,
It wasn't to be . . .
My teammates were frightened
To practice with me.
A helmet would hardly
Fit over my head.
As soon as they saw me,
The cheerleaders fled.

My sojourn with baseball
Was more of the same,
My strike zone was simply
Too big for the game.
I even played hockey
Against all advice,
I put on my skates,
And I fell through the ice.

I finally tried tennis,
But that was the worst . . .
My rackets all shattered
As tennis balls burst.
I knocked over nets
And made mincemeat of courts—
I'm starting to sense
I'm unsuited for sports.

AWFUL OGRE'S BONE COLLECTION

I'm a noted bone collector,
It's a hobby I enjoy.
I began with elf and gnome bones
When I was an ogre boy.
I spend many leisure moments
Idly trifling with my bones,
And have polished some so often
They resemble precious stones.

I have wishbones by the dozen,
Stacks of tailbones by the ton,
Bags and barrels crammed with backbones
I examine one by one.
In abundant bins and barrels,
Baskets, bowls, and cubbyholes,
I exhibit dragon toe bones
And the shoulder bones of trolls.

There's a goblin's puny breastbone
Perched upon the mantelpiece,
And a set of centaur anklebones,
A present from my niece.
There's a pair of stony wing bones
Of a gargoyle, long expired,
And the formidable jawbone
Of an uncle I admired.

There's a giant's massive thighbone
Mounted high upon a wall,
And the pinkie bones of pixies,
They're conspicuously small.
I've erected sturdy fences
Out of many bones I own,
And employed a wide selection
To construct my xylophone.

My collection's finest specimen
Is possibly unique,
An unblemished griffin skeleton,
Complete with claws and beak.
I display it in a showcase
Midst assorted rare debris—
The lock will only open
When I use my skeleton key.

AWFUL OGRE GOES TO BED

My awful day is ending,
I've ranted, roared, and raved.
At best I've been unpleasant
And greatly misbehaved.
But now I'm growing weary,
It's time to rest my head
Upon the stony pillow
Atop my rocky bed.

Good night to silent vipers
That slither in the mud.
Good night to tiny parasites
Whose touch can curdle blood.
Good night to furtive spiders
That lurk in murky wells.
Good night to loathsome vermin
With nauseating smells.

Good night to lowly rodents
That gnaw on rotting waste.
Good night to nasty maggots
That even I won't taste.
Good night to savage raptors
And beasts that claw and bite.
Good night to Awful Ogre—
Good night! Good night! Good night!

AWFUL OGRE'S AWFUL DREAM

I meander through a meadow
Moist with early morning dew.
The sun's an orange circle,
And the sky's a brilliant blue.
Bees are buzzing busily,
And roses show their blooms,
Sheep are grazing calmly,
And a peacock spreads its plumes.

Fish are splashing in a pond,
A cheerful robin sings,
Butterflies are fluttering
On multicolored wings.
I waken with a shudder.
I am terrified! I roar—
I have never had a nightmare
Nearly half this bad before.